Dinky the Dolphin

COLLINGWOOD O'HARE ENTERTAINMENT LTD

Created by Trevor Ricketts and Christopher O'Hare

Series developed by Tony Collingwood

First published in Great Britain in 2001 by HarperCollins*Children's Books*,
a division of HarperCollins*Publishers* Ltd,
77-85 Fulham Palace Road, Hammersmith, London W6 8JB.

ISBN: 0 00 710870 2

1 3 5 7 9 10 8 6 4 2

A CIP catalogue record for this title is available from the British Library.

The HarperCollins website address is:
www.fireandwater.com

Printed and bound in Hong Kong

ANIMAL STORIES

Dinky the Dolphin

Written by Joe Boyle

An imprint of HarperCollinsPublishers

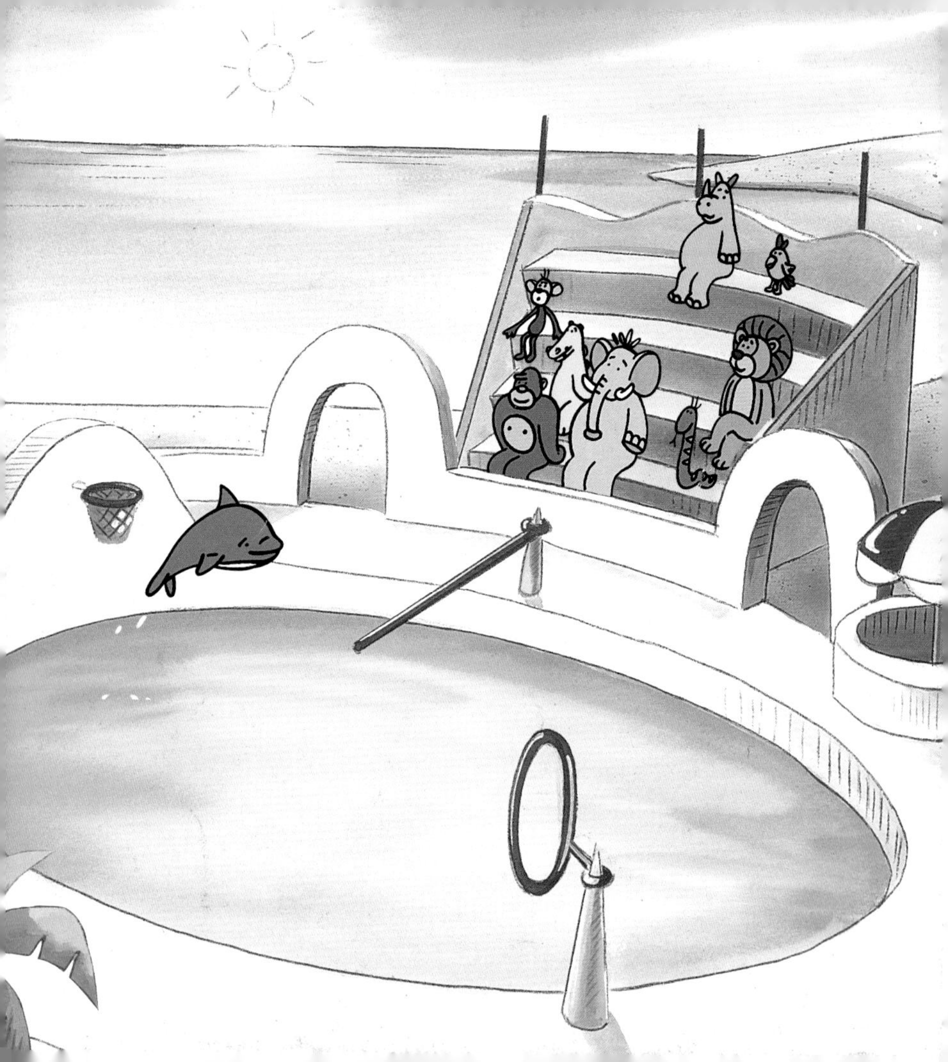

Dinky the Dolphin
Rose with the lark,
And worked every day
In a big marine park.

He'd jump through a hoop
And flip over sticks,
And crowds stood in line
To applaud all his tricks.

Orang-utan Jim
Was the boss of the show.
Dinky was his,
And he'd not let him go.

While Dinky did tricks
That were clever and funny,
Big Jim sat back
And counted his money.

Dinky's best trick
Was hitting a ball,
Which fell through a net
That hung from a wall.

And on Mondays he wore,
On a piece of elastic,
A skirt round his middle
Of shiny, red plastic

Each time Dinky leapt
From the pool in an arc,
He saw the warm ocean
Outside of the park.

He wished he was out there –
Oh, how he did wish –
Instead of performing
For buckets of fish.

Then Dinky decided
He wouldn't play ball.
He jumped out of the water
And over the wall.

Orang-utan Jim
Beat his chest with a roar.
That Dolphin made money,
And Jim wanted more.

But Dinky swam off
To the wide open sea,
Excited and happy,
And most of all – free!

Before very long
He came within sight
Of a school of wild Dolphins,
Like him blue and white.

"I know what I'll do,"
Dinky chuckled with glee.
"I'll show them some tricks,
So perhaps they'll like me."

He did his gymnastics,
And how they did stare,
As he ended up looping
The loop in the air.

But nobody cheered
Or shouted, “Hooray!”
They called him a show-off,
And then swam away.

Dinky watched sadly
As the Dolphins departed,
Leaving him lonely
And quite broken hearted.

Then, just as he thought
He'd go back to the park,
He heard a loud scream
And a Dolphin cried, "Shark!"

Now, when Sharks are hungry
Their choppers go "CRUNCH",
And this Shark clearly wanted
A Dolphin for lunch.

"Look out!" shouted Dinky,
"A Shark's on the loose."
"At last," he thought proudly,
"My tricks are of use."

Dinky shot forward,
In a brave sort of way,
And looped around Sharky
While the rest swam away.

The Shark snapped at Dinky
As they chased round the reef,
His tail only inches
From Sharky's sharp teeth.

But Dinky was clever,
And led the old Shark
To Orang-utan Jim's
Big marine park.

Then, using the trick
That he'd learnt with a ball,
Dinky whacked Sharky
Up over the wall.

Now the Dolphins are happy
To let Dinky stay.
And I'm glad to report
He's there to this day.

He leads such a happy
And free kind of life,
With a cute little Dolphin
Who now is his wife.

While Sharky has learnt
To jump and catch fishes,
Keeping one eye on Jim
Who would taste quite delicious!

The End